# BEASTQUEST

→ BOOK ONE ←

# FERNO
## THE FIRE DRAGON

ADAM BLADE

ILLUSTRATED BY EZRA TUCKER

A
**LITTLE APPLE**
PAPERBACK

SCHOLASTIC INC.

New York  Toronto  London  Auckland  Sydney
Mexico City  New Delhi  Hong Kong  Buenos Aires

*For Jamie Morgan*

*With thanks to Stephen Cole*

ISBN-13: 978-0-439-90651-7
ISBN-10: 0-439-90651-2

Beast Quest series created by Working Partners Ltd, London.
BEAST QUEST is a trademark of Working Partners Ltd.

Published by Scholastic Inc., 557 Broadway, New York, NY 10012, by arrangement with Working Partners Limited.

12 11 10 9 8 7                                        9 10 11 12/0

Designed by Tim Hall
Printed in the U.S.A.
First printing, March 2007

## ⇥ PROLOGUE ⇤

## QUEST'S END

CALDOR THE BRAVE STOOD AT THE FOOT OF the misty mountain. The knight's bronze armor gleamed in the pale morning sunlight. He gripped a heavy sword.

Turning to his squire, Robin, he used his weapon to point up the mountainside. "I'll climb above the mist," Caldor told the boy. "The dragon is close by. I can feel it. I just need to get above the mist so that I can *see* it. For the sake of our kingdom, it must be stopped!"

"Good luck, sir," Robin said in a shaky voice, as the knight turned to climb up the smooth, dark slope of the mountain. Caldor struggled to keep his footing on the overlapping plates of rock. They were as slippery as glass, but the knight was determined, and slowly but surely made his way up the mountain. He was soon lost from sight, swallowed by the eerie mist. Robin had never seen a mountainside like this before. With his master gone, he noticed how quiet it was. He shivered, although the air was warm.

Suddenly, the mountain started to shake.

Robin could feel the vibrations traveling through his feet and up his legs. He stumbled to one side and a huge shudder threw him to the ground, knocking his head so badly that his teeth clattered. There was a metallic taste in his mouth and he put a hand to his lips. Blood! What was happening? "Caldor!" Robin yelled, scrambling to his feet as the rocks shifted beneath him. "Come back!" But there was no way he could be heard above the grinding screeches that filled the air. The whole mountain shuddered and Robin froze. Was it about to come crashing down?

Robin looked up and gasped in disbelief. Two huge rocks high above him started to *move*. They stretched out slowly, their razor-sharp edges catching the sunlight. Robin flinched as they swiped through the air like giant ax heads.

Rolling out of the way, he glimpsed Caldor high above him, clinging to the dark slope of the mountain. The spiked head of a huge beast reared up behind the knight. Its face was the same color as the slippery stones of the mountain. Its eyes glinted with dark fire.

"Come down, Caldor!" Robin yelled desperately. It all made sudden, horrible sense. The dragon wasn't near the mountain — it *was* the mountain! And Caldor was barely holding on to the monster's neck! "Caldor!" Robin yelled again. But a terrifying roar drowned out Robin's words. He stumbled to his feet, his mouth open in shock.

Glancing down, Robin realized that his own situation was nearly as dangerous as Caldor's. He was standing on the dragon's tail! He wanted to run, but he was frozen with fear. And as he looked up at Caldor, he knew he could not abandon his knight. Robin could only stare in disbelief as the dragon's wings unfolded overhead, stretching out to beat the air in a deadly rhythm.

"It's taking off!" he shouted. "Caldor, quick —"

"Get back, Robin!" called Caldor, still desperately clutching the creature's neck. "Go to the city. Warn King Hugo that I have failed in my quest. Run!"

Robin had no chance to run. The dragon flicked its tail and sent him flying through the air. He hit the ground, shaking and gasping for breath, as the terrifying beast rose up into the air and disappeared into the mist, taking Caldor with him.

For a moment, Caldor's screams filled Robin's

ears. Then, to his horrified eyes, an empty piece of armor clattered to the ground beside him, scorched and smoking.

The echoes of Caldor's screams hung in the air. Then they, too, were gone.

# → Chapter One ←

## The Mysterious Fire

Tom stared hard at his enemy. "Surrender, villain!" he cried, waving his sword above his head. "Surrender, or taste my blade!"

The sword was only a poker, and his enemy was a sack of hay hanging from a tree in the heart of the wood. But then, Tom was not a knight. He was training to be a blacksmith. The closest he came to thrilling quests was when he ran errands for his uncle Henry, who worked the village forge.

Today, Tom was taking a sack of newly mended tools to Farmer Gretlin. Along the way, he had stopped in the forest to practice his sword-fighting moves on the dummy he had made a few weeks

ago. He trained whenever he could. If he ever had the chance to have a real sword fight, he'd be ready!

Tom gave the target a firm blow with the poker. "One day I'll be the finest swordsman in all of the kingdom of Avantia," he announced. "Even better than my father, Taladon the Swift!"

Tom had heard many people in the village praise Taladon's swordsmanship. But he had never seen it for himself. Tom's mother had died of a fever when he was just a baby. That same day, his father had left on a mysterious quest and never returned. As Head of Errinel village and Tom's closest relative, Uncle Henry had announced that he and his wife, Maria, would raise him as their own son.

Tom was grateful to his uncle and trained hard as a blacksmith's apprentice. But he often dreamed of leaving Errinel, just as his father had. He wanted to taste adventure for real — dreams just weren't enough anymore. But most of all, he wanted to find his father and ask him why he had left.

Tom shoved the poker back into the sack of tools. "One day I'll know the truth," he swore.

Summer was giving way to autumn, and Tom shivered as he walked beneath the shadows cast by the trees' heavy branches. It was hard-going along the overgrown forest path. Branches tore at Tom's clothes and scratched his face. Stumbling over tree roots, Tom struggled on. As he neared the edge of the woods, he smelled something strange.

*Smoke!* he thought as the sharp smell caught at the back of his throat.

He stopped and looked around. Through the trees to his left he could hear a faint crackling as a wave of warm air hit him.

*Fire!*

Tom began to push his way through the trees. Heart pounding, he forced his way through a thicket and burst into the field. The golden wheat had been burned to black stubble. A thin veil of smoke hung in the air, small flames still licked at the edges of the field. Tom stared in horror. What had happened?

A shadow fell over him. Tom looked up and blinked. For a second he thought he saw a dark, fleeting shape disappear behind a hill in the distance. Had his eyes been playing tricks on him?

"Who's there?"

Through the smoke, Tom saw a man stamping across the field. Forgetting the shadow, he hurried forward to meet him.

"Did you come through the woods?" Gretlin demanded. "Did you see anyone who could have done this?"

Tom shook his head. "No one! I didn't see a soul in the woods."

"There's evil at work here," said Gretlin, his eyes flashing angrily. "Only ten minutes ago, this wheat was as tall as your shoulders. I was working in the barn when I heard a strange noise, like a fierce wind. I rushed outside to find . . . *this*." Gretlin stared at the blackened field. "Mark my words — no ordinary fire did this. Just like no ordinary fire took John Blake's horses."

A shiver of fear went through Tom. John Blake lived at the edge of Errinel, and two weeks ago he had lost three of his horses during the night. Their bones were found the next day, in a smoking pit at the foot of the valley — roasted and picked clean. "The old ones are talking in the village," said Gretlin, shaking his head. "They say dark forces are gathering. . . ."

Tom looked around at the burned field and felt a wave of anger. Someone needed to stop this. If only he was older! *I'd do it*, he thought. *I'd stop things like this happening in our kingdom.*

"Go back to the forge, Tom," Gretlin said. "Tell your uncle what's happened here! I'm worried that Errinel is cursed — and maybe all of us along with it!"

# → CHAPTER TWO →

## A REAL QUEST

THE SUN HOVERED LOW AND PINK ABOVE THE distant hills. Villagers crowded into the market square, jostling for space. Tom had never seen the square so full of people, and they just seemed to keep coming. Tom had told his uncle Henry about the strange fire, and Henry had decided to call an emergency meeting of the whole village. Nothing like this had ever happened in Errinel before, and Tom couldn't ignore the hard knot of nervousness in his stomach. From the low murmurs coming from the crowd, he could tell that everyone else was on edge, too.

Uncle Henry stood on a wooden bench in front of the villagers. Tom waited off to the side with his aunt Maria. She looked tired and worried.

"This meeting is open," Uncle Henry announced. "Now, I've heard plenty of rumors, but let's try to deal with facts."

"The troubles get worse each day!" called John Blake. "*That's* a fact!"

"Have you seen the river?" a woman asked. "It's running so low that we will soon run out of drinking water."

"We're cursed!" an old man shouted.

"I don't believe in curses," said Uncle Henry firmly. "But it is clear that our village needs aid. Someone must go to the king and request help, while the rest of us try to figure out why this is happening."

Tom smiled. He could picture himself traveling to the city to ask for help and save his village. It was the opportunity he had been waiting for! A real adventure! He stepped forward. "*I'll* go to the palace."

There were murmurs of astonishment from the crowd and a few chuckles.

"Trust the fate of our village to a boy? Ha!"

Uncle Henry spoke quietly. "No, Tom. You're too young to take such a trip on your own. I will go as Head of Errinel."

Suddenly, a young, ragged boy, smeared in soot, pushed through the crowd. It was Adam from nearby Dreen Farm.

"Help!" gasped Adam. "Our hay barn is on fire!"

"We're all cursed!" wailed a woman.

"Gretlin! John! Take twenty men and fetch water from the river!" roared Henry. "The rest of you bring spades — if we can't quench the fire we'll bury it in mud. Quickly!"

Aunt Maria looked at Uncle Henry as the crowd

rushed to obey. "These people need you here as their leader," she said quietly.

"You can't go!" added Tom. "And who else can be spared? Harvest is the busiest time of year for the whole village."

Uncle Henry turned to Tom. "Very well. You're young and fit, and I have to let you go out into the world sooner or later. You may go to the king's palace. But you must leave first thing tomorrow!"

Tom hugged his uncle. "I won't let you down," he swore, turning to hug Aunt Maria as well. His heart was doing somersaults. He couldn't believe it. Tomorrow he was setting off for the palace on a real quest — a chance for adventure at last!

## CHAPTER THREE

## WHISPERS OF BEASTS

It was still dark when Tom began his journey. And as the sun rose, he saw that Errinel wasn't the only place in trouble. He passed fields and meadows that lay black and dead. Dry ditches traced paths where streams had once flowed.

On and on Tom walked, ignoring his tired muscles and aching feet. He was determined to get to the city and talk to the king! As he got closer to the high city walls, other people joined him on the dusty road.

Men cantered by on horseback. Families walked beside donkeys weighed down with packs. He could hear them muttering to one another. One farmer was selling sheep at the market; another hoped to get a good price for his oats and barley. But many of the weary travelers seemed to be fleeing famine and danger and, just like Tom, were heading to the palace to ask for help. Tom started to walk faster.

The city gates were open. As Tom passed through them he felt a new surge of energy. He was here at last!

He pushed his way through the narrow, crooked streets. There were tall wooden houses on each side of him and traders were standing by stalls, calling out to people to come and buy their wares. The air was muggy, the smell of cooking mingling with the market animals and the people jostling through the crowded street. Chickens squawked in cages, goats bleated loudly, and mangy dogs sniffed around the stalls for scraps of food.

Tom quickly jumped aside as someone trotted

by on a horse. It was so different from his village where everyone knew one another and stopped to say hello. Here, no one even looked at him.

Tom didn't care, though. He had one aim — and that was to get to the palace! He could see it, towering over all the other buildings at the center of the city. The sun shone on its soaring purple spires and domes of sea-green glass.

But as he reached the palace courtyard, Tom found that his way was blocked by a crowd of people. There was a long line, and it was moving very slowly toward the King's Clerk — a tubby little man sitting behind a large table, scratching on paper with the inky stalk of a feather. He was talking to a ragged old man who seemed close to exhaustion.

"Now then," said the Clerk primly. "Where are you from?"

"We're doomed," gasped the ragged man. "If the king will not help —"

"Sorry, I'm a little deaf," the Clerk apologized. "What did you say?"

The ragged man groaned. "I said, we're doomed!"

"Ah, you're from the village of Weirdoom," said the Clerk, carefully writing this down. "Where's that?"

"No, no," said the ragged man impatiently, "I mean, we're *all* doomed!"

"The village of *Wirral*doom," the Clerk corrected himself, crossing out his first entry.

"Oh, this is hopeless!" Tom said. "At this rate, I'll be here till next Tuesday!"

"I don't think we have that much time," said a stout man with a beard down to his knees. "In the West we've been hit by tidal waves. We need help to build sea barriers!"

"There are terrible blizzards in the North," said an old woman. "The whole kingdom is in danger! And mark my words — the Beasts have done this."

"The Beasts?" scoffed the stout man. "You must be joking!"

"Joking, am I?" The old woman glared at him. Her skin was lined and pale like parchment, but her eyes were a fierce blue. "It's *them*, I tell you!"

Tom frowned. Like every other child in the kingdom, he had heard tales of the Beasts. They were strange creatures, dragons and sea serpents, said to dwell in the darkest corners of Avantia — though no one had ever seen them. "The Beasts are only make-believe," Tom protested. "Stories to scare little kids."

The old woman looked at him. "If no one believes in the Beasts, how will they ever be stopped?"

"Well, I never heard any tales of them causing droughts or floods," Tom insisted, turning away from her.

"Something has happened," she said. "Something to turn them against us and destroy our land. Yes, something evil has disturbed the Beasts this time. . . ."

"What?" Tom spun back around.

But the old woman had gone.

"Did you see her?" Tom stared at his neighbors, baffled. "Where did she go?"

"Who cares?" said the stout man. "It's one less person in line."

Tom fell silent. He found himself thinking of the strange shadow he had glimpsed in Gretlin's field. Could it have been cast by a Beast? He suddenly realized that fires as big as the one at Gretlin's wheat field did not happen naturally . . . something had started that fire.

Something *huge*.

Suddenly, Tom felt another shadow fall over him. He looked up but found only storm clouds blowing in swiftly over the city.

Anything might be lurking up above the clouds. Anything at all.

## → CHAPTER FOUR ←

## THE COURT OF THE KING

TOM MADE UP HIS MIND. WAITING WAS GETTING him nowhere. If he even made it to the front of the line, his complaint would be one of hundreds. He'd come to ask the king for help and that was exactly what he was going to do — even if it meant sneaking into the palace! He struggled through the crowds and out of the courtyard.

The pale light of the moon shone down on Tom. He started to circle the palace. "What I need is an open window," he muttered under his breath. "Or an unlocked door."

Guards were posted all the way around the palace walls. By the time Tom reached the eastern gateway, manned by two guards, he didn't feel so sure of himself. *Perhaps lots of people have tried to see the king*, he thought, moving farther into the shadows. *Maybe they've been locked up in the dungeons. . . .*

Suddenly, there was the sound of running footsteps. A young, ragged lad stumbled out of the night toward the palace.

"Open the gates!" the boy shouted hoarsely. He was around Tom's age, caked in dirt. He clutched a piece of armor in one hand and a parchment scroll in the other. "I bring word from Sir Caldor. I must see the king!"

To Tom's surprise, the guards opened the gates and then rushed to help the boy, leaving the gates wide open.

*This is it!* Tom thought.

He sprinted over and ducked inside behind the guards' backs.

"Not so fast, boy," said a voice behind him. Heart pounding, Tom looked back. A guard was moving toward him, crossbow aimed. Tom had to think quickly. He was dirty, tired, and hungry from days of travel. He didn't look like he belonged in the palace at all! But he had to take a chance.

"Kitchen delivery," Tom said quietly, pointing at his rucksack.

The guard's eyes narrowed. "Aren't you a little late?" he asked, clearly suspicious.

Tom had a feeling this was a test. "Am I? Then I'd better hurry!" he said, taking a few steps forward.

The guard looked uncertain but lowered his weapon and let him pass, giving Tom a final piercing stare. This boy did seem somehow familiar. . . .

"Yeah, you'd better. And don't even think about sneaking through the front gate again—I don't care how much longer it takes to go around!" the guard shouted at the boy's back.

Tom walked forward confidently. He didn't dare look back until the guard was out of sight.

*Another close call,* he thought to himself. *Now I need to find the king!*

Sticking to the shadows and staying close to the walls, Tom cautiously explored the palace. A delicious smell of roasting meat and vegetables came wafting toward him through a door that was slightly ajar. His stomach growled. It seemed like ages since his meal of bread and cheese the day before. *The palace kitchens must be in there,* he said to himself. *My excuse already worked once. Maybe if I go in, I'll find a way of getting to King Hugo.*

"Act like you own the place," he muttered, marching up to the door. "Then no one will question what you're doing here."

Excitement and fear beat through him. Would he get away with it? All he knew was that the future of his village depended on it!

As soon as Tom walked in, he was struck by a heat so fierce it reminded him of the forge at home. Huge iron cauldrons hung over open fires. Red-cheeked maids milled about, stirring the steaming stews and laying out food on silver platters.

A huge, doughy woman bustled up to him, blond curls escaping from her lacy cap. "Ah!" she cried. "You must be the new kitchen boy the Chamberlain sent."

"What? Oh, yes, that's right," Tom agreed quickly.

"I'm Cook," the woman continued. "Thank goodness you're here! Two serving girls are off sick and the king's supper is almost ready to be served."

"The king's supper?" Tom gulped. "You want *me* to serve food to the *king*?"

"You? Don't be daft, the head usher tends to him!" Cook gave a hearty laugh. "But the king is dining with his lords and ladies of the Inner Council tonight. You shall help to serve them what little food we have left!" She wiped her nose on the back of her hand, then threw a handful of herbs into a cauldron. Tom couldn't believe the food shortages were affecting the palace. The troubles were even worse than he had imagined.

In a daze, Tom followed Cook over to where platters of food waited, ready for serving. A steward gave Tom a quick lesson in balancing the platter with his hand held high above his head. Then he turned on his heel. Tom followed him and the other servants up to the beaten-bronze doors of the royal dining chamber.

The head usher led the way inside and Tom's heart beat faster. There was King Hugo himself, seated at a long table lit by tall candles. He was surrounded by grim-faced lords and ladies. Tom felt his breath catch in his throat. He had somehow managed to trick his way into the very heart of the palace! This was surely his chance to talk to the king.

But, looking at the majestic figure at the head of

the table, Tom suddenly felt nervous. What should he say? Should he bow? What if King Hugo had him thrown into the dungeon?

*Remember everyone at home,* he told himself. *You can't back out now.*

Squaring his shoulders, he carried his platter to the far end of the table. A short, elderly man with a wispy white beard sat there. He was dressed in a gown of faded red silk, a pointed hat perched upon his head. The old man's gray eyes seemed to glow in the candlelight, as bright as the jewel he wore on a chain about his neck.

*I thought only wizards dressed like that,* Tom thought to himself.

"Well, a blacksmith would look pretty stupid in these clothes, wouldn't he?" said the old man with a smile.

Tom gasped. "You read my mind!"

"That's because I *am* a wizard," the old man

murmured, watching him closely. "But what are *you*, I wonder . . . ?"

Tom didn't have a chance to reply. The dining room doors flew open. The ragged young boy with the piece of armor and parchment scrambled inside. Two guards followed closely behind him.

"Forgive me, sire," the boy croaked. "I am Robin, squire of Caldor the Brave. I come to you at his command."

The king rose to his feet. "Greetings, Robin," he said. "But where is Sir Caldor?"

Robin's eyes brimmed with tears as he held up the piece of armor — a scorched breastplate. "He's been burned to death by a dragon. Our quest is over."

King Hugo groaned. "My bravest knight has perished," he cried in despair. "Our kingdom is surely doomed!"

## → CHAPTER FIVE ←

## SECRET IN THE FIRE

Tom could hardly believe what he was hearing. A chill ran through him. Was the king really giving up hope?

The wizard rose gravely from the table. "The Inner Council has private matters to discuss," he said. "All those with no business here must leave at once."

Two guards shooed everyone out through the dining room door. Tom hesitated — this was his chance to find out what was going on!

"Hurry up there!" the guards ordered, pushing past Tom. Tom seized his chance and doubled back to hide behind a thick pillar. He pressed his cheek against the cold stone. His heart was pounding so loudly that he was sure someone would hear it.

"Curse the Dark Wizard Malvel!" cried one of the lords. "We *must* break this evil spell he has placed upon the Beasts, before the fire dragon destroys us all!"

Dragons? *Beasts?* So it was true! A gasp escaped Tom's lips.

Robin whipped around. "Who's that in the shadows?"

"A spy!" exclaimed King Hugo.

"Please, let me explain!" Tom pleaded. Two guards lunged forward, but he leapt out of the way. A third threw himself at Tom's legs, but Tom jumped over him. "I'm only here because I want to save lives!"

"Enough!" thundered Aduro, the wizard, and everybody froze.

"What is it, Aduro?" asked the king sharply.

The wizard smiled. "There is more to this boy than you realize."

Tom stared as a small, flickering flame appeared in the palm of Aduro's hand. Aduro held his hand out toward Tom, and the flame turned violet. King Hugo looked at Tom through the magical fire, and his eyes widened.

"Why . . . this is Taladon's son!"

"Taladon!" Tom said in disbelief. "You knew my father, Your Majesty?"

"Yes, I knew him," the king said. "What is your name, boy?"

"Tom," the wizard answered for him. "As you can see, he is every bit as swift as Taladon! Your Majesty, I must speak with you and Tom alone."

King Hugo nodded to his lords and ladies. "You may go. Please treat Robin as your honored guest."

Robin bowed and joined the lords and ladies as they left the room. As the doors closed, the wizard pulled the king to one side. Tom strained to catch their conversation as they talked in heated whispers.

At last, King Hugo beckoned to Tom. Heart pounding, Tom approached him.

"Tom, our land is in terrible danger," said the king. "The Dark Wizard Malvel has hunted down the ancient Beasts and gained power over them all. Normally, they watch over Avantia and protect us all from danger. Now they have been turned against us and carry out acts of terror and destruction in Malvel's name. Even my bravest knights are unable to stop them."

So the Beasts did exist! They were real and living in Avantia!

"Who is this Malvel character?" asked Tom.

"Once, he was a good man, with a good life," said King Hugo. "But his happiness did not last, and his life turned sour."

Aduro took up the story. "He hoped to make it sweet again through magical means. He searched out forbidden knowledge, wisdom, and power dating back to the Dawn of the Beasts, that our ancestors decreed no one should possess."

Tom's mouth felt dry. "And he found that knowledge?"

"Or it found *him*," said Aduro mysteriously.

"Why don't you catch Malvel?" Tom asked. "Then you could force him to undo his magic."

"As long as Malvel controls the Beasts, we cannot harm him," said Aduro. "We only have the power to free the Beasts one at a time, and return them to good. But we mustn't let the people of Avantia know the Beasts really exist. These creatures can only be at peace if they're left to themselves."

"Malvel's evil powers make the Beasts almost unstoppable," the king continued. "Ferno the Fire Dragon is burning all our crops. And the other Beasts — sea serpents, ice beasts, mountain giants, and more — are causing floods and avalanches elsewhere in Avantia. They will ruin our kingdom,

unless we can set them free from the enchantment. That is why I sent Sir Caldor to unlock the dragon's charmed collar." He gave Tom a large silver key. "Only this will undo the lock."

Tom turned the key over in the palm of his hand. Despite its size, it was very light.

"The key was created by Aduro, but can only be put to use by a warrior," the king murmured. "Your father once served me — now I ask you to do the same. Aduro's magic has shown me the strength and goodness within you, a match for any knight in my kingdom."

A shiver of excitement traveled up Tom's spine.

The king leaned forward. "Will you risk your life on the Beast Quest?"

"I will," Tom said without hesitation. He had never been more sure of anything in his life. "Whatever it takes — *I will!*"

## CHAPTER SIX

## GATHERING STORM

TOM WOKE EARLY THE NEXT MORNING IN THE royal guest bedroom. Excitement swept through him and he jumped out of bed. New clothes and a silver chain-mail vest had been laid out on a wooden chest near the door.

His heart pounded as he slipped on the dark trousers and woolen, long-sleeved vest. Then, with a thrill of delight, he tried the chain mail on for size. It was beautifully made and fit him perfectly. Over that he wore a plain gray tabard to hide the chain mail. After all, his quest *was* a secret one. Tom smiled proudly as he looked at his reflection in the mirror. No one would guess that the king had given a simple blacksmith's apprentice such a vital mission.

Suddenly he felt a moment of doubt.

*Can I really succeed where the bravest knight in the land has failed?* Tom wondered to himself.

"Yes, you can," came a soft voice behind him.

Tom turned with a start to find the wizard Aduro at the door. He was holding a sword and a wooden shield.

"You may think you are an unlikely hero," Aduro went on. "But in these strange times, all things are possible."

"I suppose they are," Tom agreed with a smile. "Are the sword and shield for me?"

"Let's find out." Aduro tossed the sword over to him.

Tom caught it by the hilt. It matched his grip perfectly and felt far lighter than the blacksmith's tools he'd used for practice. "This is the sword for me!" he cried.

Now Aduro passed him the polished wooden shield. It was well crafted, but very plain. Tom remembered the knights at the king's coronation with their bright, colorful shields and felt a twinge of disappointment.

"Appearances can be deceiving," Aduro smiled, reading Tom's thoughts. "On your quest, you will find allies in the strangest of places and in unlikely forms. But you have a wise heart, boy. Trust your instincts."

"I'll try. But tell me . . ." Tom hesitated. "I have always thought that my father left me to go on a quest of his own. Is that true, Aduro?"

"So I have heard," the wizard said evenly. "And I believe his quest goes on, even now."

"Then he had a reason for leaving me alone," Tom realized. "And I shall do all I can to help save the kingdom — and to make him proud of me." He paused, looking into Aduro's eyes. "Do you think I will ever see him again?"

"All things are possible," said Aduro quietly. "Now, I have other gifts for you. Firstly . . ." He took a parchment scroll from his pocket. The scroll was just like the one Robin had been holding the night before.

As Aduro unrolled it, Tom saw it was a map of the whole kingdom. Tom stepped closer for a better look, and the map came to life! Trees and hills and mountains rose up from the paper, standing as tall as Tom's thumbnail. Cautiously he reached out to touch one of the white mountains in the north. His finger came away glittering with frost.

Tom looked up at Aduro, startled. The wizard nodded at the map.

"Look closer," Aduro commanded.

Now Tom saw tiny twisting paths spring up like veins on the pale parchment. They slowly spread across the map toward a large mountain in the southwest, dark and unwelcoming.

"The Fire Dragon's mountain," Tom guessed.

"Yes." Aduro held up the silver key Tom had been shown the night before. A loop of leather cord had been threaded through the top, and Aduro hung the key around Tom's neck like a medal. "Only if you set Ferno free can I begin to put right Malvel's evil."

"I will do all I can," Tom promised.

"Now, you must go," Aduro said. "Your horse waits outside."

Tom picked up his sword and shield and followed Aduro out to the stable yard, where a groom stood with a jet-black stallion. Tom had seen many horses and ponies come into his uncle's forge, but he had never before seen one as beautiful as this.

The stallion whinnied in greeting. It had a white mark the shape of an arrowhead between its eyes. Two leather bags hung down on either side of its saddle.

"The stallion's name is Storm," said Aduro. "He is young and fast."

Storm pushed his nose against Tom's shoulder and looked up at him.

Tom beamed. "I think we'll get along well, Storm," he said as he grabbed the reins and swung himself up onto the horse's back.

He looked down at the wizard. "What will happen to my village? They are relying on me for help."

"A cart is on its way there with food and water," said Aduro. "The driver will tell your uncle you have been sent on a special errand for the king — and that you will return as soon as you can."

Tom patted Storm's neck. "Thank you, Aduro — and good-bye!"

"Farewell, my young friend. All our hopes go with you."

Tom nodded and clapped his heels to Storm's sides. Storm cantered away, out of the palace courtyard and into the hectic city streets. Storm's hooves clattered on the cobblestones as he swerved around carts and passersby. Tom saw the city gates looming up ahead. His heart pounded with excitement. Soon he would be on his own. "Faster, Storm!" he urged.

Storm galloped out through the gates. As they headed toward the grassy plains, Tom gave a wild whoop. This was it! His adventure had begun!

Charging along on horseback, Tom felt any doubts he had slip away. Not only was Storm the fastest horse Tom had ever ridden, but he seemed to understand exactly what Tom wanted him to do. He slowed down at the slightest pull on the reins and sped up the second Tom touched him with his heels. He and Storm would be fine, so long as they stuck together.

By late afternoon they had reached the edge of the grassy plains. A vast forest stretched out before them. It looked dark and mysterious, but the map showed that the quickest way to the dragon's cave was to cut straight through the woods.

"Come on, Storm," Tom said, carefully guiding the stallion through the trees. "We'll go this way."

The trail twisted and turned through the silent forest. The trees seemed to press in closer and closer. Branches clawed at Tom's hair and scratched his cheeks.

Pulling his sword from its sheath, he dismounted and started hacking at the undergrowth to clear a path.

Tom suddenly heard a rustling noise and stopped still.

"Who's there?" Tom called.

No answer.

Pressing on, Tom sliced through a thick tangle of brambles. Did the trail get any clearer up ahead? Taking hold of Storm's reins, he pushed his way through the thicket.

A set of gleaming yellow fangs suddenly snapped in his face.

Tom leaped back with a shout of alarm. A wolf! Its gray fur was matted, its amber eyes wild. Strings of drool hung from its jaws. Its huge paws were like clubs and ended in lethal claws.

Tom staggered back against Storm.

Gray fur bristling, the wolf bared its teeth and crouched down, ready to spring!

## CHAPTER SEVEN

## THE FOREST OF FEAR

Storm pulled away from Tom and reared up, kicking out with his front hooves. Tom threw himself into the bushes by the side of the trail. But the wolf didn't attack Tom. It growled at something that was crashing through the undergrowth.

Suddenly, three soldiers smashed their way into the clearing, their eyes glinting fiercely through the slit in their helmets. The wolf advanced toward them and its growl grew angrier.

"We'll teach that girl and her vermin to steal from our master!" snarled the first soldier, aiming his crossbow at the wolf's head.

"No!" Tom scrambled up from his hiding place just as the soldier shot an arrow. Thinking quickly, Tom threw his sword. It spun through the air and sliced the short, heavy arrow in half before plunging into a tree trunk.

"Another poacher! Get him!" One of the soldiers charged at Tom, sword raised. But the wolf threw itself at the man's legs, knocking them out from under him. Outraged, the other two soldiers charged toward Tom.

Tom grabbed Storm's reins and swung himself onto the horse's back. Lying low in the saddle, he rushed at the men with the wolf at his side, sending them running. Steering sharply, he pulled Storm back around and wrenched his sword from the tree trunk. He rode toward the soldiers once again, scattering them into the woods. The wolf pulled ahead, and Tom and Storm galloped after it.

The wolf moved like the wind, only slowing once it had led Tom and Storm a safe distance from the soldiers. Tom eased Storm back down to a trot.

And then they saw the girl.

She was tall and skinny, dressed in breeches and a dirty blouse. Her black hair was short and messy, and her face was red with scratches. In her hand, she clutched a bow. A quiver of arrows was slung over one shoulder. As she crouched to welcome back her wolf, her green eyes narrowed at Tom.

"It's all right. I'm not going to hurt you," he promised, pulling back on the reins until Storm stopped. "My name is Tom," he said, dismounting. "You can trust me."

The wolf trotted over to him and pushed its nose into Tom's hand.

The girl visibly relaxed and grinned at him, her smile full of warmth. "Well, if Silver trusts you, so will I."

"Where did you get him?" Tom asked.

"I found him injured on a hunting trip to the North," the girl replied. "I nursed him back to health, and we've been friends ever since." She stepped forward, took his hand and shook it firmly. "My name's Elenna."

"Were those soldiers after you?" asked Tom.

Elenna frowned. "My father's a fisherman — but now that the river has dried up, there's nowhere to fish and nothing to eat." She sighed. "Silver and I came here to hunt rabbits. But the soldiers thought we were after the local lord's deer."

A noisy crashing came from somewhere behind them. Tom looked around in alarm. "Quick! We'd better get out of here!" Putting his foot in a stirrup, he swung himself onto Storm's back. "Come on!" Seeing Elenna hesitate, he grabbed her hand and helped her scramble onto the horse behind him.

Storm snorted and leaped forward into a gallop. They raced through the woods, Silver bounding ahead of them.

"Hold tight!" Tom shouted to Elenna as Storm swerved between the trees.

"I am!" she gasped, clutching him. "Hey!" she exclaimed suddenly. "Is this *chain mail* you're wearing? You're too young to be a knight, aren't you?"

"I'll tell you everything once we've lost the soldiers," Tom said, glancing behind him anxiously.

To his relief, the soldiers were no match for Storm's swift hooves and Elenna's knowledge of the forest. Soon their shouts died away into the distance and Tom eased Storm back down to a walk. "I think we're safe," he said, turning off the trail.

A small stream was bubbling nearby. The stallion plunged his head into the cool water and drank deeply. Silver joined him.

Elenna looked at Tom. Then, without asking, she opened the horse's saddlebags, revealing Tom's sword and shield stowed there. "Village boys don't carry weapons this fine," she said. "What's all this about, young knight?"

Tom hesitated. Something told him he could rely on this girl, and Aduro had told Tom to trust his instincts. He had to tell her the truth. "I am on a quest," he said. "A quest for the king."

"The *king*?" Elenna echoed, sliding down from the horse.

"The Beasts have returned," he said.

Elenna raised her eyebrows. "You don't *really* believe in the Beasts, do you?"

"I'm serious!" he snapped. "You did ask what was going on."

"All right," she said. "I just thought you were teasing me." She paused. "See, I always thought the Beasts were more than just a story. . . ."

"They are," Tom told her, gravely. "Ferno the Fire Dragon is under an evil spell and I've got to stop him from burning the kingdom's crops. . . ."

By the time he'd finished, Elenna's eyes were large and serious "So *that's* what's been happening!" she breathed.

Tom frowned. "You believe me? Just like that?"

"It all sounds unbelievable," Elenna replied. "But it explains so much! I knew nothing natural could make an entire river dry up overnight. . . ." She bit her lip, and then nodded as if she had reached a decision. "I think I'd better come with you."

"You can't!" Tom protested. "It's too dangerous!"

"Not as dangerous as you trying to stop a dragon all by yourself!" Elenna shot back.

"But what about your family?" Tom asked.

Elenna shrugged. "I often stay out hunting for days at a time. They won't be worried." She lifted her chin. "So, let's go and find this dragon then."

Tom half smiled as he remembered the wizard Aduro's words: *On your quest, you will find allies in the strangest of places, and in unlikely forms. . . .*

The wizard was right.

## CHAPTER EIGHT

## DAWN OF THE DRAGON

"THIS IS THE LAST OF THE FOOD," SAID TOM, passing Elenna some bread. The air was cold, and the first streaks of dawn were just shooting across the sky.

"Should we save it?" she wondered.

Tom stuffed some more into his mouth. "You can't fight dragons on an empty stomach."

"Stale bread makes a rotten last meal," Elenna decided, gnawing at the crust. "But it would make an even more rotten victory feast!"

For two days and nights Tom and Elenna had traveled, until they reached the outer limits of Avantia. Now they sat atop a hill. While Storm rested his muzzle on Elenna's shoulder, Tom opened the map and studied it closely. The fire that had warmed them through the night was dying, but it still gave off enough light to see by.

"Let me look!" cried Elenna, running to kneel next to Tom. Ever since he had first shown her the magical map, Elenna had been fascinated by it.

"We're very close now," he said. "There should be a river near here. But I haven't seen anything."

"The Winding River! Of course!" Elenna said excitedly. She pointed through the mist to a massive stack of boulders piled up across a valley. "Perhaps the river has been dammed up by all those rocks."

"By the dragon? I wonder . . ." Tom pressed his finger against the parchment, and sure enough, it came away bone dry. "I think you're right," he said. "Come on. Let's take a closer look."

They lit a torch with the last dying embers of the fire, then set off, following the dry riverbank to the base of the mountain. The mist was thicker here. It was impossible to see what might await them at the top. They walked slowly, squinting through the fog for any signs of life — or a way up. Tom noticed a promising foothold and stepped forward, torch in hand. Storm threw back his head and nickered, and Silver's hackles rose in warning.

Tom stopped dead. The key seemed to tingle on the cord around his neck, and his stomach felt knotted with nerves. Silver pressed himself up against Elenna's legs, while Tom stroked Storm's rough mane for comfort.

"I'm not surprised the animals are spooked," Elenna said, taking an arrow from her quiver. "It does look pretty scary."

Tom passed the torch to Elenna as he retrieved his sword and shield from Storm's saddlebags. With weapons at the ready, they leaned in closer.

The rock was black and glassy. In the flickering

light of the torch, it almost seemed to shine like dark scales.

Silver let out a long, low growl. "Shhh, not now, boy," Elenna whispered soothingly, without taking her eyes from the rock. The usually obedient wolf only growled louder. Elenna turned around to give a hushed reprimand, but the words stuck in her throat. Now she could see what Silver had been growling about. A dark shape was flying toward them — fast. "Tom!" she shouted in alarm, "Get down!"

Before Tom could obey, he was knocked to the ground by a roaring wind. Using all his strength, he rolled onto his back in time to catch a glimpse of the largest creature he had ever seen passing right above them. It was traveling at incredible speed. The gale slowed to a gusty breeze as the creature slowed, circling. It was the dragon! Tom stumbled to his feet, not taking his eyes off it.

"Storm and Silver found safer ground," said Elenna, pointing to a sheltered spot close by. "If we follow them, we'll have better footing."

Tom nodded. "We'd better hurry, I don't think we have much time."

A dreadful roar echoed all around them. The mountainside shuddered, pitching an avalanche of rock down the slope. Tom held up his shield to protect them as he and Elenna ran toward Storm and Silver. Boulders were tumbling down on all sides, dangerously close.

Morning sunlight glinted on black-red scales as Ferno the Fire Dragon settled slowly on the mountain. Tom covered his ears as Ferno let out another echoing roar. Silver howled, while Storm skittered backward.

"What are we going to do?" Elenna shouted.

The dragon towered over them, his unfolded wings like huge, jagged sails blocking out the

sky. His head was coal-black and spiky; and tight around his neck was the enchanted collar, held in place by a golden padlock that glowed with a strange, magical light.

"We *have* to remove that collar," said Tom. "Then Ferno will stop serving Malvel and go back to protecting the kingdom."

"But that dragon is as tall as a mountain!" Elenna cried, clutching Silver for comfort as he edged forward to join them. "How will we ever reach the collar?"

Slowly, the dragon lowered his head, sniffing the air, eyes bright and blood-red. His dreadful gaze fell on them. Tom stared deep into the monster's eyes and felt a terrible paralyzing fear. Somehow he was able to rise to his feet and pull out his sword.

Ferno was faster. Uncoiling his huge forked tail, the Fire Dragon lashed it out like a deadly whip. But before it could strike, Silver bravely pounced on the end and snapped his teeth into the scaly flesh. With a screeching cry, Ferno jerked his tail up into the air with Silver clinging to it.

Ferno swung his tail viciously this way and that, until the wolf could hold on no longer. Thrown like a stone, he landed with a thump and lay still.

"Silver!" cried Elenna, sprinting toward him.

"No, Elenna!" Tom shouted. "Don't!"

But Ferno had noticed Elenna's sudden movement. He opened his massive mouth and let out a furious roar.

*Ferno is going to attack Elenna!* Tom realized in horror. *She doesn't stand a chance!*

## CHAPTER NINE

## FINAL COMBAT

IN DESPERATION, TOM SWUNG AROUND AND whistled to Storm. The jet-black pony galloped over. "Come on, boy!" Tom cried, leaping into the saddle. "We've got to save Elenna!"

Elenna had just reached Silver's motionless body as Ferno prepared to strike. Tom touched his heels to Storm's sides and the horse leaped forward. They galloped across the hillside. Over the pounding of the stallion's hooves, Tom could hear the roar building in the dragon's throat.

"Elenna, get down!" Tom shouted.

She turned and saw the dragon's open mouth. She gasped and froze in fear.

Tom drew all his weight backward and pulled on the reins. As Storm skidded to a stop, Tom hurled himself from the horse's back. He landed badly. Pain shot through his ankle, but he didn't have time to stop. There was a boulder just behind Elenna. If they could both just get behind it . . .

But it was too late.

Ferno's eyes narrowed to fierce slits. With a roar, he blasted an enormous fireball. Ignoring the stabbing pain in his ankle, Tom dove in front of Elenna and threw up his shield. The deadly flames rained down around them, fire singeing the hairs on Tom's arms, catching the rim of the shield. He saw the dragon shrink back as the fire rebounded at it. But Tom knew Ferno would attack again, and quickly. . . .

The inferno died down until only thick black smoke remained. The dragon pulled his head away, roaring in anger. Tom's shield was badly scorched, but at least it was still in one piece. He swung it over his shoulder and helped Elenna to her feet. "Are you all right?"

"I think so, thanks to you and Storm," she said. "But what about Silver?"

"We can't help him until we've stopped the dragon," Tom said. "If that thing roasted us, nobody would be left to look after Silver."

Elenna sighed and nodded. "We *have* to get that collar off! But how?"

Tom whistled for Storm. Neighing loudly, the horse tore through the curtain of smoke and skidded to a stop beside them.

"Well done, boy, you were very fast," Tom told him. "But now you've got to be even faster." He gave Elenna his sword, checked that his shield was secured over his shoulder, and scrambled onto the saddle.

"What are you going to do?" she asked.

"I'm going to free the dragon!" Tom cried. "Wish me luck!" With a whoop, he dug his heels into Storm's sides. Eyes stinging from the drifting smoke, he pushed Storm into a gallop. The horse shot like an arrow toward the dragon.

Ferno loomed up ahead of them. Fighting to keep his balance and wincing at the pain in his ankle, Tom scrambled into a crouching position in the saddle. The horse was racing right for the beast's gigantic, outstretched wing. As Storm ducked down to gallop underneath it, Tom leaped into the air and landed on top of the wing. It felt hard as stone, but blood-warm. The dragon flapped its mighty wings in slow, staggering sweeps. Tom felt a gale whip up around him, tugging at his hair, teasing tears from his eyes. Struggling to find a handhold, he felt himself start to slip.

With a furious hiss, the dragon thrust its head up close to inspect its unwanted passenger.

Seeing his chance, Tom ducked under its craggy chin and threw himself at the enchanted collar around its neck.

"Got you!" he cried, slipping an arm through the golden hoop of the giant padlock. Under here he was safe from the dragon's fire — but already the dragon was shaking its head from side to side, trying to send Tom falling to the ground.

Tom's arm felt as though it was about to be yanked out of its shoulder socket, but he gritted his teeth and held on. With his free hand, he pulled the charmed key from around his neck and tried to jam it in the lock.

Ferno roared in anger. The noise was deafening. Tom's arm burned with terrible pain and the world started spinning about him. *I can't pass out now!* he thought desperately. But the key slipped from his fingers and fell to the ground far below.

*"No!"* he yelled. The dragon threw its head forward and twisted its neck, but still Tom held on. How could he get the key back?

Suddenly, through the drifting smoke, he saw Elenna charging toward him on Storm. She was

still holding her bow and arrow, and it looked like she meant to use it. But she was aiming at *him*!

"Your shield!" she yelled. "Tom, use your shield!"

"What are you doing?" he shouted in confusion. He quickly shifted his grip and raised his shield — just as Elenna let loose the arrow.

With a *thunk,* he felt its arrival in the scorched wood. Tom peered over the top of the shield.

There was the charmed key, tied to the end of the arrow.

The dragon lunged forward and blew another deadly fireball at Elenna, but Storm was quicker. He thundered over the scorched grass, carrying her away from danger.

With the key in his hand, there was still hope! With a final burst of energy, Tom pushed the key into the lock. It turned with a smooth click.

The collar glowed brilliant blue for a moment, then both the collar and the padlock faded away.

Tom couldn't believe it. *I did it!* he thought. *I really did it!* Then, in the same split second, he realized that now he had nothing to cling on to but the key. With a shout, Tom found himself plunging to the ground. . . .

But as Tom fell, the dragon brought its wing under him, providing a safe but uncomfortable landing. All of a sudden, Tom was engulfed in a sea of black, unsure of what was happening. Ferno tipped his wing, sending Tom tumbling down the leathery surface to land softly beside Elenna and Storm.

"I can't believe it!" gasped Elenna, handing him back his sword. "Ferno broke your fall!"

"Did he?" Tom asked, still bewildered. Then Silver bounded through the smoke toward them.

Elenna gathered up the panting wolf in a hug, but her green eyes were still troubled. "What about Ferno?"

Tom turned to face the Beast. Ferno squatted

among the hilltops, his red eyes fixed on them. But this time, Tom wasn't afraid.

"Thank you," Tom called out softly. "You're free now."

The dragon shook out his massive wings. Then he took off into the sky. Flurries of air whipped Tom and Elenna's hair back from their faces.

Ferno swooped over the dry riverbed and lashed out with his tail at the barrier of boulders. The huge rocks shattered and a wave of water surged down the riverbed like a caged creature released.

"This was just for starters, Malvel!" Tom shouted into the sunlight as the last of the mist melted away. "I won't rest until *all* the Beasts are free again!"

Ferno drank deeply from the water. Then he threw back his spiky head and roared. The fire dragon took flight for the far horizon, leaving a rainbow of fire across the blue sky.

## CHAPTER TEN

## THE BEGINNING

"WHAT NOW?" ASKED ELENNA.

Tom wasn't sure. "I suppose we should go to the palace and tell the king what's happened. We've done it! We've set Ferno free!"

"I still don't quite believe it," Elenna admitted with a nervous laugh.

"Me, neither!" said Tom. "But it's true!" It felt like his blood was roaring through his body with as much power as the water surging through the valley below. He grabbed Elenna in a joyful hug.

Suddenly, she sprang away from him, pointing to one of Storm's saddlebags. "Look, Tom!"

Something inside was glowing. Light spilled out from under the flap of the bag.

Tom quickly reached inside, pulled out the magical map and unrolled it. A puff of smoke escaped the tiny palace marked on the parchment. It rose up before him, growing steadily larger. Storm nickered, and Silver bared his teeth.

"Is it Malvel?" Elenna asked, her voice only a whisper. "Has he come to get us?"

"I don't think so," Tom told her, both perplexed and enthralled, as the smoke took the shape of someone very familiar. "No, it's all right. It's the wizard Aduro!"

"Well done, Tom," said the wizard's ghostly image. "And you, too, Elenna. Avantia owes you both a great deal."

"How are you doing this?" Tom asked. "How can you see us?"

"Remember the jewel I wear around my neck?"

The wizard smiled. "With that, I can see throughout the entire kingdom."

"Then you saw everything that happened with the dragon?" Elenna asked.

"I did," said the wizard. "You both showed great courage and determination. You are proving to be true heroes. But your journey is not over — I must reveal to you the details of your next quest."

Tom nodded, a tingle of excitement creeping down his spine.

"Malvel will not give up his quest for destruction after just this first defeat," Aduro continued.

"We won't give up our quest, either," said Tom firmly. Elenna nodded.

The wizard smiled. "Those are brave words. But first, Tom, the scales must fall from your eyes."

"What does he mean?" asked Elenna.

Tom shook his head, baffled. Then he followed the wizard's gaze to something glinting in the crook of a scorched branch of a nearby tree. Ignoring the aching of his overworked muscles, he scrambled up to retrieve it.

It was a red-black dragon scale. "Wow," he murmured. "What a souvenir!"

"It is more than that," said Aduro. "You have earned it by winning your battle with Ferno. Now, if you place it in your shield, it will deflect all kinds of heat!"

Elenna pointed to a scorched groove in the center of the shield. As Tom reached out his hand toward it, the groove gave off a bright, ruby-red glow. Tom pressed the scale into place and the wood seemed to heal around it, leaving it glinting like a jewel in the light.

"Your shield is a little less plain now, eh, Tom?" Aduro smiled, before his face turned serious. "But there is no time to waste. You must follow the path on the map to the next stage of your Beast Quest!"

Tom and Elenna gazed at the map. A snaking green path was starting to form on the parchment, stretching across to the Western Ocean.

"What about our families?" Tom asked.

"Don't forget that you are Taladon's son," the wizard said. "Why do you think your uncle Henry tried so hard to keep you safe at home, young Tom?"

"My uncle knew about the Beast Quest?" Tom asked in surprise.

"No. But he knows you have a great destiny to fulfill," Aduro answered. "Your families will accept your absence more easily than you might expect. I will ease their worries and make sure they know you are safe."

"We understand," said Elenna.

"I must leave you," said Aduro. His image began to dissolve like smoke in the breeze. "Good luck, my friends."

"Wait," said Tom urgently. "What about my

father?" He wanted to tell him about his battle with Ferno, to earn his respect and to make him proud. But most of all, he simply wanted to know his father was alive and safe. "Will I *ever* know what happened to him?"

"You will learn a lot on this quest, Tom," said the wizard mysteriously, his words echoing into the air. "Farewell. . . ."

The image of Aduro faded slowly, smoke disappearing into the sky. All that was left was a sparkle in the air where the wizard's eyes had been.

Tom looked again at the parchment map. The green path led to a tiny image of a sea serpent, rising up and splashing with its tail.

Suddenly, he felt his blood chill and his mind darken. He pictured himself struggling in foaming black water against a huge, writhing foe. He could almost feel huge ivory fangs closing down around his body and sense fierce eyes staring into his very soul.

He shook his head and the visions faded. Imagination? A warning from Aduro? Or could it be Malvel himself placing images in his head — a dark prophecy of the dangers to come. . . .

"Tom?" Elenna's worried voice broke his concentration. "What was it? Did you see something?"

Tom nodded, unable to speak.

"Was it horrible?" she asked curiously.

Tom looked toward the horizon. "There are dark times ahead," he said gravely. "But if we proved anything today, it's that there's nothing the two of us can't face."

Elenna smiled at him. Together with Storm and Silver, they set off down the hillside, heading west.